Naomi in the Middle

Naomi in the Middle

by Norma Klein

pictures by Leigh Grant

The Dial Press · New York

Library of Congress Cataloging in Publication Data
Klein, Norma, 1938-   Naomi in the middle.
[1. Brothers and sisters—Fiction. 2. Family life— Fiction]
I. Grant, Leigh, illus. II. Title.
PZ7.K678345Nao   [Fic]   74-2878
ISBN 0-8037-6080-9   ISBN 0-8037-6081-7 (lib. bdg.)

To Judy Blume

Contents

Pussy Willows for Mommy   3

Bobo Plans to Run Away   8

A Drooping Snowman   12

Valentines   20

In the Middle   27

A Hippopotamus in the Bathtub   31

A Loom for Bobo   36

White Whales Smile   41

The Middle of the Night   47

Naomi in the Middle

Pussy Willows
for Mommy

This is how we found out. Daddy came home from work and gave Mommy a bunch of flowers. They were pussy willows. He kissed her on the cheek. She gave him a hug. She said, "Darling, how sweet!"

Bobo said, "Pussy willows aren't sweet! They don't even smell."

Bobo is nine. Her real name is Barbara, but we call her Bobo. She is very smart and usually quite bossy.

She knows a lot of things I don't. That's because I'm only seven. I'm Naomi and that's what they call me—just Naomi. I wish I had a nickname, but no one ever thought of one.

I went over and began to stroke the pussy willows. They have a nice soft feeling even if they don't smell. They feel like a kitten's nose. Once we visited this farm and there were kittens just born in the hay. Their eyes weren't even open yet. They had noses like pussy willows.

"Did Mommy tell you the big news?" Daddy said. He was smiling. He looked excited.

Mommy turned pink. She does that sometimes. She said, "No."

Bobo said, "What's the big news?" She looked like she didn't think it was going to be something good. "Come on—tell us."

"We're having a baby," Daddy said.

"You're having a baby?" Bobo said to Daddy.

"Don't be silly," I said. "How can he? He's a daddy."

"Daddy means our family will have a new baby," Mommy said. She had her shorts on because every Friday afternoon she plays tennis. She didn't look like she was going to have a baby.

"When will it be?" Bobo asked.

"The end of May," said Mommy.

I gave Mommy a hug.

"Thank you, darling," she said.

"There're getting to be a lot of children in this house," said Bobo. She sat down for her supper.

"What's wrong with children?" Daddy said.

"Two is enough," said Bobo. "You don't need three."

"We'll stop at three," said Mommy. "Don't worry, Bobs."

"You'll probably have a hundred," said Bobo.

I laughed, and milk came out of my nose. Bobo always makes me do that by saying something silly when I'm drinking my milk.

"Is the baby there now?" I said, looking at Mommy's belly. It wasn't big and round, the way Mrs. Weeks, our shop teacher's belly was when she was pregnant last year.

"It's there," Daddy said, "but it's tiny."

"How big?" I said.

"One inch," Daddy said.

I thought of that baby one inch long swimming in Mommy's stomach with all that room, like a little goldfish in a big bowl.

"Do you think it will really be so bad?" I said to Bobo as we got into our pajamas.

"We'll see," was all Bobo would say.

Bobo Plans
to Run Away

In three weeks it will be Christmas. This is the last Christmas with just the five of us: Mommy, Daddy, Bobo, me, and Alice, who is Bobo's rat. Alice is not too nice, but Bobo loves her. Bobo has to tear paper every day for her cage. Sometimes she lets her loose and has her run all over her body and sniff at her.

"What do you hope it is?" I said to Bobo.

I had been at my music lesson. I take recorder les-

8

sons from a lady in our building, Mrs. Curtis. She lives on the other side, but it's just on two, so you can walk up.

"A girl, of course," Bobo said.

"But we have two girls. I'd rather have a boy."

Bobo made a face. "Boys are noisy. They knock things down."

"So? Girls do that too, sometimes."

"Boys do it more."

If it is a boy, I hope it's like Hubbell Williamson. He is the nicest boy in our class. If I wear the kind of boots that go on over your shoes, he says, "Can I help you take them off?" When we make big buildings out of blocks, he will help, even with things like Coney Island that are a lot of work.

"As long as it's not twins," Bobo said. "I hate twins."

"What's so bad about twins?" I said. There are twins in our playground, Christos and Angelica, and they are not so bad. Christos knocked out all his front teeth so he looks funny, but he is not so bad.

"They are twice as bad as one regular baby in every way," Bobo said. "If they have twins, I will leave home."

"Where would you go?" I said.

9

"To Grandma's," said Bobo.

I don't think Grandma would let Bobo stay. Where would she sleep? There's only one bedroom. I bet Bobo wants to go there because Grandma has a color TV and we don't. That's not fair. I hope they won't let her.

Mommy came in to run our bath. "Bubble, pine, or regular?" she said.

"Reg," said Bobo.

Bobo never likes bubble anymore. She used to. I can only have a bubble now if I have it by myself.

"Will he have a bath with us if he's a boy?" I asked Bobo when we were in the bath.

"Maybe."

"Then he might put his penis in our vagina," I said. "That's what boys do."

"They don't do that till they're much much older," Bobo said.

"Sallie Cartwell says her brother does it right now and he's four."

"The people in your class are crazy," Bobo said. She began to wash her ears with the fish sponge. She says it's a fish. To me it looks more like a turtle.

A Drooping Snowman

"The baby can do lots of things now," Mommy said. She was helping me make a snowman. We were in Central Park. Bobo was home with her best friend, Fiona Page. Daddy was baby-sitting.

"What can he do?" I said.

"He can kick," Mommy said.

"Can you feel him?"

"Not yet. Maybe next month I'll be able to."

12

Our snowman was not so good. He was drooping because all of a sudden the sun had come out.

"What do you say to a cup of cocoa?" Mommy said.

"I say good," I said. The tips of my toes were cold, even though I had my fur-lined boots on.

I held Mommy's hand going home. I said, "Bobo only wants a girl. . . . She says she'll leave home if it's twins."

"I doubt it will be twins," Mommy said. "But a girl would be nice."

"Three girls would be too many," I said.

"No, it wouldn't," Mommy said. "It would be nice."

"It would be the same thing all over again," I said.

"No, it wouldn't," said Mommy. "It would be different. Look how different you and Bobo are."

That's true. I hope the baby isn't bossy like Bobo is.

"Bobo said the baby got there by Daddy putting his penis in you," I said. "Is that right?"

We were coming to our lobby. Mommy said, "Yes, that is."

"I wonder why it has to happen in such a funny way. Is it always like that?"

"Yes."

"I don't think I'd like it," I said. "I wish I could lay an egg."

"When you're old enough, you'll like it," Mommy said. "Most people do. It's just like hugging someone. But part of them is inside you."

I thought of that. That didn't sound so bad. "I wish the word penis wasn't so funny," I said.

"It's not, darling."

"I wish it were a pretty word."

"There's nothing wrong with it. People just feel embarrassed saying it, so they think it sounds funny."

"Do you feel embarrassed saying it too?"

"When I was little I did."

Mommy when she was little looked like me. I've seen a picture of her in our album. She had short curly hair. She was a little fat. She had a rabbit she liked. There's a picture of her in a pink coat that I like best. It was her Easter coat, I think. I hope this Easter we can go to the Children's Zoo again and go down the rabbit hole the way we did last year.

When we got upstairs, Bobo and Fiona were in the den. They were sitting under the piano with a lot of toys and stuff. As soon as they saw us, they began to yell. They jumped up and shut the door. "You can't come in! You can't come in!" Bobo yelled.

Mommy opened the door anyway. "What's going on in here?" she said.

Bobo looked mad. "We're doing something private," she said, glaring at me. "We don't want *her* to see."

"Bobo, cut that out right away," Mommy said. "You keep this door open. If Naomi wants to join in with you, you let her."

I didn't even feel like joining in. Bobo always thinks her dumb games are so much fun. Well, they're not; they're stupid. I can think of better games any day.

"She'll wreck it!" Bobo moaned. "We don't want her." She and Fiona began shutting the door again.

"Oh, let them!" I said crossly.

But Mommy yanked the door open again. "Bobo, this is the worst rudeness I have seen yet, ever! Now shape up right this minute." She marched into the den. "What are you doing under the piano, anyway?"

"It's a game," Bobo snarled. "It's Marsha's birthday, and we're celebrating it." I could see they had donuts and paper cups of punch there.

"Who is Marsha?" said Mommy.

"She's our imaginary friend," Fiona said.

"She's *not* imaginary," Bobo said. "She's *real.*"

"Well, what're all those dolls doing hanging from the bottom of the piano?" Mommy said.

"They're playing," Bobo said. "Marsha likes them."

"Those are our new doll-house dolls," I said. "We got those for Christmas." I came closer. "And you got them all dirty!"

Mommy sighed. "Bobo, what in the world is wrong with you?" She knelt down and pulled the dolls off the piano. "It's filthy under here. Why hang dolls under a piano? Use your *head*, darling!"

"I *do* use my head." Bobo was really mad. She began chewing on the ends of her hair the way she sometimes does.

"Now clean this whole mess up this *minute*," Mommy said. "You've gotten crumbs on the rug and everything."

"*She* better help me," Bobo said, meaning Fiona.

"Of course she will."

I went into our room. I sort of like it when Mommy gets mad at Bobo, though I know that's mean. Once I went and peeked in, and they were crawling around cleaning everything up. "You're supposed to be helping me," Bobo was saying to Fiona. "You're just sitting there."

17

"I'm your guest," Fiona said. But she began helping.

Boy, Bobo is bossy even with her own friends!

Just to make Bobo feel better, I decided to make a present for Marsha since it was her birthday. I scraped some snow off the windowsill and added a little maple syrup to it. "Bobo, this is for Marsha," I said. "It's pudding."

Bobo looked at it. "Pudding! It looks like mush!"

She and Fiona began to roar with laughter. "Ooh, that looks yukky," Fiona said. "Marsha would throw up if she ate that."

"Fiona, it's five o'clock," Mommy said. "I think it's about time you went home."

Fiona just lives in the building next to ours, so she can walk home alone. "Can she stay for supper? Please, pretty please?" Bobo said, jumping around.

"No, she may not," Mommy said.

"But we promised Marsha," Bobo said.

"Sorry, Marsha," Mommy said. "How old is this famous girl, anyway?"

"Nine," Fiona said.

"Ten," Bobo said.

"That means she's ninety," I said. "Nine times ten."

"Marsha, you're a grandma," Mommy said. "I never knew."

"Oh quit it! She is not! She's six feet tall, and she has golden curls."

"Wow!" I laughed.

"If you think she's a grandma, you must be pretty dumb," Bobo said.

"So long, Fiona," called Mommy.

" 'Bye," Bobo said. She ran out to the elevator. "Marsha, you come back here," we heard her say.

After Fiona went home, I sat down at the table and tasted my pudding. It wasn't so bad. It was a little mushy. Mommy came in and while she was waiting for supper to be ready, we did some coloring together. I hope even when the baby comes, Mommy and I can still go off together and do things like we did this afternoon with no one else in the family along. That's the way I like it best.

Valentines

I'll bet you didn't know that babies can have hiccups even before they're born.

We were sitting making valentines—Bobo, Mommy, and me. Bobo makes just a few and she works on them very hard. I like to do the kind where you mostly press them out. I give one to every person in my class, even Pamela Stevens, who is not that nice, and Nicki Gross, who is sort of wild. Mommy says that is more fair. If you leave people out, they feel bad.

Mommy was making a big valentine for Daddy. She was drawing a picture of him. It looked sort of like him, but she made him have so much hair he almost looked like a girl. Suddenly she gave a jump. "Oops," she said.

"Did he kick you?" I said.

"I think he's having hiccups," she said.

She let me put my hand on her belly. I could feel this little tiny jumping feeling. "I wish I could scare him," I said.

"Why?" said Mommy.

"Then his hiccups would go away."

"He hasn't got anything better to do anyway," Bobo said. Her valentine was really beautiful—it had real lace and a heart cut out of red felt. It was for Fiona. I don't have a best friend that is that much my best friend the way it is with Fiona and Bobo. I have Samantha Klieg, but it is not the same. I wouldn't work that hard on one valentine just for her.

He must be bored in there, I thought, doing nothing, just kicking. I wish I could remember what it was like. I guess nobody does. This boy on my school bus said he did remember, but nobody believed him. It might be just like being asleep, but without having dreams. I'm glad you only have to do it once. One thing I don't like—that they hit you when you're just born. Mommy says they do it to make sure you're all right and can breathe. But I don't see why they have to hit you. They could just say very loud, "Are you all right?" Mommy and Daddy never hit us. They don't believe in it. Mommy said people who hit their children should go to jail.

Bobo sighed. "This is probably the best valentine I ever made," she said.

Bobo is so good at everything. I wish she wasn't. The only thing she can't do that I can do is play the recorder. That's because she plays the cello.

Mommy said, "I have to practice, girls. You can finish up by five."

I don't like hearing Mommy practice. It's just scales, up and down. She is a singer, and once Daddy took Bobo and me to see her in this opera called *The Marriage of Figaro*. It was hard to tell it was her. She came out in a very pretty dress with flowers with a lot of other ladies. It sounded quite good. But when she practices, it just sounds like: ba ba ba ba ba.

"I'm going to make a valentine for Mommy," I said.

"*I* already did," Bobo said.

"Can I see it?"

"Okay." Bobo showed it to me. It was really pretty.

"Are you going to make one for Daddy too?"

"Sure."

I decided to make one for Daddy too. I wrote, "To my sweetheart Daddy" on a pink heart.

Bobo said, "He's not *your* sweetheart. He's Mommy's."

"Well, I can still call him that."

"I bet you wish you could marry him when you grow up," Bobo said scornfully.

"I do," I said. "But I know you can't. Because he can't be married to two people at once."

"Even if he wasn't married to Mommy, he couldn't marry *you*," Bobo said.

I looked around for the scissors. "Didn't you ever wish you could marry him?" I said.

"Oh, I guess . . . when I was really little," Bobo said.

Suddenly we heard someone outside the window shout, "Hey, knock it off, lady!" We looked at each other. In the den Mommy was going: "Ah ah ah ah ah!"

"Do you think he means her?" I said.

Bobo nodded. She looked sort of scared. "He must be trying to sleep or something."

"But it's only four o'clock in the afternoon!"

"Maybe he's trying to work. He must think she's noisy."

We were quiet a minute. The man yelled again. "Shut up, lady!"

"He's not so polite," I said.

"Do you think Mommy heard him?" Bobo said.

"I don't think so, or she would have come out. Should we tell her?"

"That would hurt her feelings," Bobo said.

That's true. We went back to doing our valentines. "Maybe he doesn't mind anymore," I said.

But then the man yelled again. "Listen, lady, pipe down!"

Bobo went to the window. She yelled really loud, "You pipe down yourself!"

The man didn't say anything.

I began giggling. "Good work, Bobo."

Bobo smiled. "She can sing if she wants. It's a free country." She sat down again. "I know what he means, though," she whispered. "It *is* sort of noisy."

"She always stops at five thirty," I whispered back.

At five thirty I had finished all my valentines, even one for Grandma. And that man never yelled again. Bobo must have scared him.

In the Middle

Last night Bobo said something mean. She said, "Now you will be a middle child."

"What is so bad about that?" I said.

"Middle children never like it," she said. "They hate it. They wish they were first or last. The best is to be first."

Bobo just says that because she is first. She wants to think everything she does is best. We were at

27

Grandma's house watching this special on color TV. I asked Grandma, "Were you the first child?"

"Oh goodness, no," Grandma said. "I was the last out of seven."

"So you weren't middle?" I said. "You were last. Bobo says that's good."

"There wasn't anything that good about it," Grandma said. "Nobody paid any attention to me. They just babied me. I was fat and they always came over and squeezed my cheek and said, "Googy-googy-googy!" She reached over and squeezed my cheek to show me how it was. It hurt.

"That hurts!" I said.

"It was worse when they did it," Grandma said. "Being seventh was awful."

"Well, not that many people have seven anymore, I guess," I said.

"Thank God," Grandma said.

"Why do you say Thank God if you don't believe in God?" I asked Grandma.

"Oh, it's just an expression," she said. She began laying out her tennis stuff. Grandma plays tennis three times a week, indoors in winter. She is better than Mommy. She says Mommy can't play net.

When Mommy was taking her bath Saturday night,

I came in and sat on the toilet. I said, "Was it good being first?" Mommy was first in her family like Bobo. She only had one brother.

"Yes," Mommy said.

"I wish I could be first," I said. "It's not fair. Some people are always first and it's just because they were born that way."

"Daddy was a middle child," Mommy said.

I hadn't remembered that. Daddy has two brothers, Uncle John and Uncle Jeremiah. Uncle John is divorced and lives in Boston. Uncle Jeremiah is studying to be a doctor. He is six feet four. Once when I was very little, he stepped on my foot, and I was very proud that I didn't cry because he was so tall.

Mommy let me wash her back. I squeezed the water over her and she said it felt good. She has funny crinkly hair between her legs that looks like moss. She says I will have it too. I hope it doesn't itch.

When Daddy was putting me to bed, I said, "Did you mind being the middle child?"

He said, "Why should I? The first one has to be so responsible and do everything right, and the baby is always a baby. But the middle one can go and mind his own business and do whatever he likes."

I guess that's what I'll do: mind my own business.

A Hippopotamus
in the Bathtub

Tomorrow is April Fool's Day. I have to think how to fool Grandma. I think I might tell her there's a hippopotamus in her bathtub.

"That's no good," Bobo said. "She'd know that wasn't true."

That's so. It has to be real enough to really fool the person.

When Bobo came home from school the next day, I

said to her, "Bo . . . guess what? Mommy had twins!"

"Oh, quit your old April Fool stuff," she said. "How could she? She's not even having the baby till May."

It's very hard to fool Bobo, almost impossible because she always remembers that it is April Fool's Day. It's better with people who don't remember.

Mommy is getting quite fat. She says that when she takes a shower, she can't see her feet. That must be funny. You'd wonder—are they still there? Of course, then, after you got out of the shower, you could check just to be sure.

Mommy takes a nap after lunch every day. On weekends she lets me nap next to her. But she really falls asleep and I never do. When I was a baby, I used to take a nap every day but not anymore. Having a baby in you must be like having a package that you can never set down. It would be easier to sit on an egg. Except then you could never go places. But you could wrap the egg in an electric blanket. Then it would stay warm till you got back.

"How many children will you have?" I asked Bobo. She was at Daddy's desk doing her homework.

"None," she said. "I'm not even getting married."

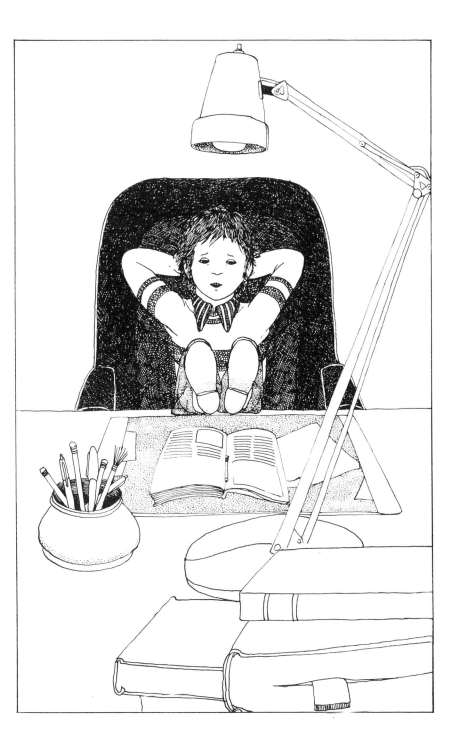

"Not to anyone?" I said. "Not even if you met the nicest person in the world?"

"I'm the nicest person in the world," Bobo said, "and I can't marry myself."

"Oh, Bobo!" Imagine marrying yourself. You would stand next to yourself and the minister would say, "Do you want to marry yourself?"

I want to marry someone. But I want to live right near Mommy and Daddy the way Grandma lives near us now. I want to visit them every day. If something goes wrong, they can come over. They can be baby-sitters if I have a baby.

"I might adopt a child who's nine years old," Bobo said. "Until then they are just pests."

Bobo is so mean sometimes for no reason, just to be mean. She knows I'm not a pest. Maybe when I was little I was, but not anymore.

I made the worst face I could think of to her back, but she didn't see me.

"I'm not a pest, Bobo," I said. "That's not even *true.*"

"You used to be worse," Bobo said.

For supper we went to Grandma's house the way we always do on Friday. Grandma was in the kitchen.

"Grandma," I called, "why is there this big pile of mud on your living-room floor?"

Grandma came running in with this very worried expression. "Where?" she said, looking around. "I didn't notice it. Where is it?"

"April Fool!" I yelled, jumping up and down.

"Oh, my goodness!" Grandma laughed. "I was never so scared. You really fooled me, Naomi. You little devil!"

I bet even Bobo never fooled anyone that much, *ever*.

A Loom for Bobo

Daddy and Bobo have a birthday on the same day: May 13. It's funny, in a way, two people in one family being born right on the same day. Mommy says it was just a coincidence. That means it just happened for no special reason.

Mommy and I went to get Bobo her present at Gimbel's. She was at her cello lesson, so she didn't know. Bobo's friend Fiona is staying over tonight. Her parents are getting divorced, and her Mommy has to go away for a little while. She can sleep in this folding bed we have.

"I'm glad you and Daddy are not getting divorced," I said.

"You know, we're lucky, darling, to have such an extremely nice dad."

I took Mommy's hand. "We will never divorce him because he is so nice and we love him," I said.

"We are lucky to have him," Mommy said.

"But you wouldn't have married him if he hadn't been the nicest person you ever met," I reminded her.

"That's true," she said.

It is hard picking a present for Bobo; she is so fussy. Mommy wanted to get her a loom so that she could weave things. "It looks very complicated," she said.

"Bobo will figure it out," I said.

If I was Bobo, I would have a Kiss Me Baby Tender Love doll with its own trunk of clothes, but Bobo is not like that. She doesn't especially like dolls. She never did, even when she was little.

"I could get her a zither," Mommy said.

"What is that?" I asked. I kept looking through the glass at these beautiful presents. There was one I liked

a lot—a mouse playground with a slide, a seesaw, and a bench to sit on.

"It's a musical instrument," Mommy said.

"But she has her cello."

"That's true," Mommy said. "I think I will get her the loom."

We had the present sent so that Bobo wouldn't know.

"Will you get something for Daddy?" I asked.

"Daddy is hard," Mommy said.

"Harder than Bobo?"

"Much harder. But this year I know what I'll get him."

We went up to another floor and this is what Mommy got: a special bag that you could put your tennis racket in. I think he will like it. Suddenly Mommy gave a jump.

"Did the baby kick you?" I said.

She nodded. "He has a hard kick. So did you."

"Did I kick more than Bobo?"

"Much more. Bobo just lay around and daydreamed the whole time."

That is just like Bobo; she would. "We should get the baby a present," I said. "He is almost nine months old."

"Well, not really," Mommy said. "You don't count the age till he is born. But that's a nice idea. Should we get him a mobile?"

"We could get him a Baby Tender Love with its own trunk of clothes," I said. "Boys like dolls too, you know."

White Whales Smile

I hope Mommy gets thin again. You never saw anyone so fat as she is now. Her face is not so bad, but the rest of her is huge. I would hate to always have such a fat Mommy, like Sheila Munth's mommy who wears a size eighteen dress.

There is one other very bad thing. Mommy has no more lap. You can't even sit on her during Sunday breakfast. I don't do that so much anymore, but I like to sometimes and now I can't; there's no room.

"It will come back," Mommy said.

I hope it will. I have to sit on Daddy's lap, which is good, but not the same. Mommy's lap is softer. It's more like a living-room chair. Daddy's is like a dining-room chair.

"Is this aquarium day?" Daddy said.

Bobo was in the corner weaving on her loom. She yelled, "Yippee!" Bobo loves doing things that have to do with animals or fish. "I want to take Alice," she said.

"Bobs," Daddy said, "don't be silly, what would a rat do at the aquarium?"

"She would look at things. She never leaves this old house. She's bored from morning till night."

"How do you know?" I said.

"She told me." Bobo will just lie at times. Everyone knows rats cannot talk or look smart the way dogs can. In fact, Alice isn't smart or pretty or anything. She smells, even right after you clean her cage.

"Alice and I will have a nice long nap at home," Mommy said.

At the aquarium we looked at the white whale a long time. Whales must be happy. They have a very happy smile on their face all the time they are swim-

ming. Bobo says that is not a real smile, but an expression.

"They might be very mad, but they would still look like that," she said.

I think they are happy because their tank is so nice; they have so much room to swim in. They can even swim upside down. It's much nicer than for lions and tigers who can just walk up and down.

Sharks smile too. They look very friendly, though I guess they aren't. They have lots of teeth, little sharp ones, one after the other. It's funny to be standing there and have a shark swim right by you, just one inch away. But there were other fish in with the shark, big turtles and some other ones. There was one odd thing: two fish were hanging on the bottom of one turtle. I thought they were tired and just wanted a ride. But Daddy said they were cleaning the turtle. I wonder why he doesn't sit down or lie on his back so they can do it well. It must be hard to do it while he is swimming.

I wonder if the baby in Mommy's stomach feels like those fish, just swimming around, back and forth. Of course now that he is big, he doesn't have so much room. Mommy says when there is no room left, he has to come out. He has to be born, whether he wants to or not. He wouldn't fit anymore.

I wonder if babies know it when they are being born or if they are surprised.

When we got back from the aquarium, Grandma and Mommy were having tea.

"I wish I could remember being born," I said. I took a cookie off the cookie plate.

"Being born!" Grandma said. "I can't remember anything that happened before I was twenty years old. I can't even remember what happened yesterday."

"Oh, Grandma!"

"Really," Grandma said. "I mean it."

"Well, I can remember everything," Bobo said. "I can even remember when *you* were born," she said to me. She took a sip of Mom's tea. Bobo says she likes tea, but I bet she just does it to be grown-up.

"You weren't even two then," I said.

"I wore a red dress with a pocket shaped like a dog that had a tongue hanging out." Bobo said.

"You know, she did!" Daddy said. "Amazing, Bobs."

"She just remembers because we have a photo of it in the album," I said. I ran to get the album and showed them. It showed Grandma, Mommy, and Bobo all standing together. Bobo looked sort of like a boy, she had such short hair.

"Well, I can remember it anyway," Bobo said. "And when we got home there was that fussy lady that yelled at Daddy."

Mommy giggled. "Mrs. Prince," she said.

"She was supposed to help us with the baby," Daddy said, "but she wouldn't let us near you, Naomi."

"She said, 'This is *my* baby,' " Mommy said. "Remember that?"

"She sounds like a great big boss," Bobo said. "Don't have her this time."

"This time we have two fine girls to do all that with us," Daddy said, winking at me.

"Bobo is a great big boss anyway," I whispered so just Grandma heard. She reached over to hug me.

The Middle of
the Night

Bobo and I sleep in the same room. The baby is going to sleep in a room that was called a den. It had Mommy's piano in it and Daddy's desk, but now Mommy's piano is in the living room and Daddy's desk is in the dining room. We hung the mobile over the crib. It's the same crib Bobo and I had. It's still good, Mommy said.

Usually I sleep through the night. Sometimes I have

a bad dream, and if it's really bad I go into Mommy and Daddy's room. Or sometimes I have to go to the bathroom. But that's all. But one night Daddy came in and woke us up. He said Mommy's baby was coming, and we had to go to Grandma's.

We had our bags all packed. We ran in to look at Mommy. She was just sitting on the bed. She had her clothes on. She didn't look any different. But she closed her eyes and said, "Hi, kids!"

"Is it hurting?" I said.

"It's okay," Mommy said.

I hope it doesn't hurt coming out. Some babies just slide right out, even in elevators or taxi cabs. I hope this one waits till they get to the hospital.

Daddy was on the phone calling Grandma.

Bobo said, "This is nine days too soon."

"You were early too, Bo," Mommy said. "Naomi was born right on the day they said. That's unusual, though."

We got on our coats. It was really dark, the middle of the night. I don't think I was ever up so late before. I felt very excited. I held Bobo's hand. It felt cold.

"Don't forget the lollipops!" Mommy said to Daddy.

It's funny. You have to eat lollipops when you have

48

a baby. It makes it easier. I wouldn't mind that. Daddy gave us each one.

"*We're* not having a baby," Bobo said.

"It's on the house," Daddy said.

Grandma was in a shocking pink bathrobe. That is her favorite color—shocking pink. My favorite is blue and Bobo's is black. I think she just picks black because no one else does.

"Call as soon as you know!" Grandma said to Daddy. Then they left.

"We woke you up in the middle of the night, Grandma," I said.

"No, you didn't," Grandma said. "I wasn't asleep yet. I was up reading."

Imagine someone still being up in the middle of the night, at two in the morning. "Weren't you scared?" I said.

"No, I like the nighttime," Grandma said. She got out our sleeping bags.

"I feel too excited to sleep," I said. "I don't think I can."

"I'm going to make you a very good drink," Grandma said. "It will make you sleepy."

We all went into the kitchen, and Grandma made this drink for all of us. It was hot milk with sugar and a little rum. You had to pour the rum from a little brown pitcher.

"I'm drunk!" Bobo said, crossing her eyes. She can do that.

"You can't be," I said. She was just showing off.

Outside a few people still had lights on. Maybe they were up reading like Grandma.

We got into our sleeping bags.

"Bo?" I said.

"What?"

"I hope it doesn't hurt Mommy coming out."

"Oh, they give you a shot," Bobo said. "You go to sleep and when you wake up, it's all over."

I hope it wasn't born in the taxi cab.

I fell asleep, but about three seconds later Grandma came running in yelling, "It's a girl."

Bobo lifted up her head and muttered, "Oh, no! Another girl!"

"You said you wanted a girl," I told her.

"Everyone in our whole *family* is a girl," she said. "You, me, Mommy, Alice . . ."

"Grandma," I added.

"I never heard of so many girls," Bobo said. "Except for Daddy—poor thing."

"Well, he grew up in a family of boys," Grandma said, "so maybe it's a nice change for him."

After breakfast we spoke to Daddy on the phone. He said, "She looks just like you, Naomi . . . piles of light curly hair and big eyes. She's a darling."

I was a cute baby, that's true. Bobo wasn't. She had no hair till she was one year old. "Did it hurt coming out?" I said.

"Not a bit. I held Mommy's hand, and she was awake the whole time."

"Didn't she even have a shot?"

"No, she didn't want one . . ."

"I got drunk," Bobo said. She was on the other extension.

"On what, Bobs? Gin?"

"Rum and milk! It's good."

"She didn't really," I said.

"I'll see you later," Daddy said, laughing.

"What's her name going to be?" I asked.

"Probably Zoe."

"You said Belinda."

"We changed our minds. We wanted to name her after Grandma."

After we hung up, we ran in. "Grandma, did you know the baby will be named after you?" Bobo said.

Grandma was having her whole wheat toast and tea. She said, "Yes, isn't that silly? What a name to foist on a child!"

"I like it," I said. I hope I don't get mixed up and call the baby Grandma; that would really be silly. Grandma let me climb into her lap. Usually she says she is not the lap type. She kept on drinking her tea. "Are you excited, Grandma, about the baby?" I asked.

"So-so," Grandma said. "I'm not big on babies, to tell the truth. I never was. They're too little and cuddly."

"That's just what Bobo says."

"I like them when they get big and complicated like you and Bobo."

"I'm not complicated," I said. "I'm simple."

"You're just right for me," Grandma said. She kept sipping her tea and holding me till Bobo came in and said it was her turn.

About the Author

Norma Klein grew up in New York City and received a B.A. from Barnard College and an M.A. in Slavic languages from Columbia. After her marriage in 1963 she began devoting full time to writing, which she has done ever since. She has published numerous short stories, two adult books, and several books for young readers, including *Mom, the Wolf Man and Me* and *Girls Can Be Anything*.

Ms. Klein lives in New York City with her husband and their two young daughters.

About the Artist

The illustrator of a number of books for young readers, Leigh Grant grew up in Greenwich, Connecticut. She earned her B.A. at Hollins College in Virginia, her B.F.A. at Pratt Institute, and has studied at various schools in Europe, including the Sorbonne. She now lives in Connecticut, where she enjoys horseback riding, sailing, and skiing.